# A GIFT FOR MAMA

"Mother's Day is coming and Sara refuses to *make* another gift for Mama. No matter what, she will find a way to buy the fancy satin slippers on display at the Bata Shoe Store.... Sara toils in secret, afternoons after school, until she has earned the big sum of nine zlotys and proudly presents the glittering slippers, with unexpected results.... Hautzig writes with such warmth and fluency about the people and the times that she turns the tale into something special. Gifted Diamond's splendid illustrations do that too."

—Publishers Weekly

"Moving in its depiction of loving relationships within a serene Jewish family."                    —*School Library Journal*

ESTHER HAUTZIG

# *A Gift for Mama*

ILLUSTRATED BY DONNA DIAMOND

Puffin Books

*I would like to thank Bob Blackburn and the Printmaking Workshop*
*for their encouragement and support. D.D.*

PUFFIN BOOKS
A Division of Penguin Books USA Inc.
375 Hudson Street   New York, New York 10014
Penguin Books Ltd, Harmondsworth, Middlesex, England
Penguin Books Australia Ltd, Ringwood, Victoria, Australia
Penguin Books Canada Limited, 2801 John Street, Markham, Ontario, Canada L3R 1B4
Penguin Books (N.Z.) Ltd, 182–190 Wairau Road, Auckland 10, New Zealand

First published by The Viking Press 1981
Published in Puffin Books 1987
5 7 9 10 8 6 4
Text copyright © Esther Hautzig, 1981
Illustrations copyright © Donna Diamond, 1981
All rights reserved
Printed in the United States of America
Set in Times Roman

Library of Congress Cataloging in Publication Data
Hautzig, Esther Rudomin.      A gift for Mama.
Summary: Sick and tired of making presents for various holidays and occasions, Sara decides that for
this Mother's Day she will do something different.
[1. Gifts—Fiction.   2. Mother's Day—Fiction]   I. Diamond, Donna, ill.
II. Title   [PZ7.H289Gi   1987]      [Fic]      86-30347      ISBN 0-14-032384-8

*With happy memories of*
*Grandmother, Margola, Eli,*
*and our vanished world*

*A Gift for Mama*

# Chapter I

SARA WAS SICK AND TIRED OF MAKING PRESENTS. AND Mother's Day was coming. For birthdays and for Hanukkah, for anniversaries and for Mother's Day, Sara always had to make a gift.

Mama said that the best presents were handmade presents. Papa said the gifts his Sara made were the best gifts of all. The lumpy pillows Sara made when she was little were still propped up on the sofa. Mama and Papa still used the linen handkerchiefs with crooked hems Sara had made.

Every picture Sara made for a special occasion hung in her parents' bedroom or in the study or in the kitchen. Some pictures even hung in the dining room. All the stories she wrote and illustrated were on the bookshelves, next to the leather-bound books stamped with gold.

Sometimes Sara was even sick and tired of *looking* at her presents. Yet Mama and Papa loved them better than all the beautiful store-bought gifts they received from other people. They always told her so.

Mama also said, "When I was growing up, I always made presents for my family. It's a tradition you should follow."

"Yes, yes, family traditions are important. Especially since our Sara makes such lovely presents," Papa would add, smiling.

Well, this year Sara decided that she was definitely not going to follow family tradition. She did not collect scraps of fabric and paper before Mother's Day. She did not press leaves or flowers between the pages of her heavy *Grimm's Fairy Tales* book. She did not do any of the things she had always done before a special day. For

## A Gift for Mama

Mother's Day she absolutely would not make another pillow or pincushion or picture. She wouldn't even make a card. This time she would buy a present, just like a grown-up.

Papa bought Mama presents. Mama bought gifts for Papa. And they bought gifts for Sara, too. This time Sara would do just what they did.

Sara knew exactly what she would buy for Mama. Shiny black satin slippers, trimmed with blue leather. She had seen them in the window of the Bata Shoe Store on Broad Street, her favorite street in all Vilna. She had gone window-shopping there with her friend Rebecca.

"Look, Rebecca, aren't these slippers beautiful? The black ones, in the middle of the window, the ones with the blue leather trim?"

"Oh, yes, they are beautiful, Sara," Rebecca answered, "but did you see how much they cost? Nine zlotys! We could go to the movies eighteen times for the price of this pair of slippers!"

"Really, Rebecca?" Sara was terrible in arithmetic so she did not doubt that Rebecca was right. Nine zlotys was a fortune—especially if she thought of seeing eighteen movies for the price of one pair of slippers! But they

were beautiful, and they would make a perfect gift for Mama.

Mama had a black satin robe with blue cuffs and collar. Papa had given it to her for her last birthday in June, but she had never worn it. Ever since Sara could remember, Mama had worn an old red flannel robe and ancient, scuffed red slippers.

How Sara wished that Mama would get all dressed up! She wished Mama would wear the shiny robe, or lacy dresses, and hats with feathers, and a fancy cape. Just like a movie star.

But Mama loved to paint and to make clay bowls, and she wore an old smock when she worked. She loved to cook, and she wore a white apron over plain dresses when she rolled out the dough for twelve-layer Napoleon cakes.

"Mama, why don't you ever wear the shiny black robe that Papa gave you?" Sara asked one morning during breakfast.

"I will, Sara. When I get new slippers, I will."

So Sara was sure that Mama would like the satin slippers. Mama could not say, as she often did, "Oh, you could make them better yourself!" Whenever Sara admired a scarf or a handkerchief or a pillow in a store window, Mama would say, "Oh, Sara, you could make that better yourself!" Sara could knit and sew and embroider. She could do all sorts of things, but she was not a shoemaker—and Mama had to know *that*!

But Sara had a problem. Sara's family wasn't poor, but Sara herself had no money. How would she ever get nine zlotys? Mama and Papa did not believe in giving Sara an allowance. If she wanted something, she asked for it. Sometimes Sara got it, and sometimes she did not.

Once, when she asked for an allowance, Mama said, "What is it you need money for?"

"I may want to buy candy on the way home from school."

"But we always have candy at home."

"Well, I might want to buy a magazine," Sara said.

"But you have subscriptions to both children's magazines, in Polish and in Yiddish."

That was true. She got both magazines every month. And there was always candy in a pretty blue bowl on the dining room sideboard. Mama had made the bowl, and she kept it filled with delicious sour balls and bonbons. All Sara and her friends had to do was take some or ask for some. Mama almost never said no, except just before a meal.

When Sara went to see a movie at Cinema Mars with Rebecca or with her cousins, Mama and Papa gave her money for the movie ticket. They gave her extra money to buy chocolates from the candy lady in the theater. They gave her money to give to the beggar who always sat on the corner.

For Hanukkah, Sara got Hanukkah *gelt*—money that she immediately spent on movie trading cards for her collection. She always hoped that she would get new pictures of Shirley Temple or Deanna Durbin, her favorite movie stars.

And so Sara had no savings, she got no allowance, and she had no money to buy a Mother's Day gift.

# Chapter II

SARA DECIDED TO TALK TO HER AUNT MARGOLA. Margola wasn't just an ordinary aunt. She was Sara's special friend. Margola was Mama's younger sister, and she was only ten years older than Sara.

*Maybe she will know how I can get nine zlotys to buy the slippers for Mama,* Sara thought.

Margola studied at the university, near Sara's house, and she often came to visit after classes. The day after

# A Gift for Mama

Mama and Papa had a fancy party, she always came with her friends. They would eat the leftovers from the party—the delicious herring salads, smoked salmon, and cheese spreads. They finished the twelve-layer Napoleon cakes filled with vanilla cream, and the miniature fruit tarts. They said Mama made fancy pastries better than anyone else in all Poland!

Since Papa was leaving for a business trip to Warsaw on Monday, Mama and Papa had a big party on Sunday. Sara knew that Margola and her friends would come on Monday after classes. And they did. They hung up their coats and university caps, dropped their books in the front hall, and went into the dining room with Mama. Sara grabbed Margola's hand and pulled her into her own room.

"Margola, Mother's Day is coming soon. This year I will *not* make a present for Mama. I want to buy one, just like a grown-up!"

"But, Sara, you make such lovely things. Mama loves them all."

"Well, this year I am not going to. I'm old enough to buy a gift for Mama. But I have no money!"

Sara's eyes filled with tears. Sara cried when she was

sad, and she even cried when she was happy. No one in her family minded. Mama seldom cried, but Papa cried easily, like Sara, when he was sad and also when he was happy. They were all used to each other's tears.

Margola did not fuss over Sara. She just asked, "Why don't you speak to your papa?"

"I can't ask Papa. Don't you know he went away this morning? Besides, he'd want to know why I need the money. He knows Mama only likes handmade gifts from me, and he wouldn't want to upset her. I just won't make a gift *this* year. Please help me."

"But, Sara, you know I'm poorer than a field mouse. I don't have an extra zloty in my purse," Margola said. "What is it you want to buy? How much will it cost?"

"Well, I saw beautiful black satin slippers in the Bata Shoe Store. They'll match Mama's black satin robe." Tears were streaming from Sara's eyes. "They cost nine zlotys!"

"Oh, my goodness, Sara, that's a lot of money! Let's both think about it for a while."

Margola left Sara's room and went into the dining room. Sara wiped her eyes, blew her nose, and followed Margola. Margola's friends—Mira and Grisha, Dina and

Janek, Bronia and Sasha—were sitting at the table, piling food on their plates.

The beautiful tablecloth that Mama had designed and embroidered was on the table. A bowl Mama had made was filled with fresh flowers just like those embroidered on the tablecloth. Everything looked as elegant as it did on Sunday night when Mama and Papa had their party.

"What were you two whispering about?" Mama asked.

Before Sara had a chance to answer, Margola said, "Oh, nothing much. I was helping Sara with her homework. You know how much trouble she always has with arithmetic."

*Margola always knows what to say or do,* Sara thought. *She will certainly come up with a solution to my problem.*

Margola and her friends were talking to Mama, telling her what was happening at the university, joking, asking questions about Mama's pottery classes and about Papa's business. They wanted to know why Papa had gone to Warsaw. Was he meeting foreign businessmen again? Would he import more machinery and appliances from Sweden and England? Sara loved their loud voices and

questions and laughter. She was amazed at how much they ate while they talked. How quickly food disappeared from all the serving platters!

As she looked around the table, Sara noticed that the scarf around Mira's shoulders had a huge rip. The elbows on Dina's sweater were almost worn through. Grisha's and Janek's shirt collars were frayed. When Sasha and Bronia moved their chairs away from the table, Sara could see an enormous hole in Sasha's left sock. There was a long run in Bronia's stocking.

Suddenly an idea flashed into Sara's mind.

"Margola, I've got to talk to you again," she whispered. She tried to pull Margola back into her own room.

"Not now, Sara, we have a late afternoon lecture at the university," Margola whispered back. "I'll come again on Wednesday afternoon when your mama goes to her pottery class. Then you and I can talk alone."

Mama kissed Margola good-bye, and she hugged all Margola's friends.

"Raya, your food is the most delicious in all Vilna!" Dina said to Mama.

"It was wonderful!" Janek added.

Mama smiled and took a little bow. "You can stay and have some more."

"We have to go now, but I wish we could all live and eat here always!" Sasha rubbed his stomach and grinned.

"Yes, yes!" they all chorused.

Margola kissed Sara good-bye. Sara kissed her back, and she kissed each of Margola's friends on both cheeks. As they were leaving, she called, "I wish you could stay with us forever!"

# Chapter III

ON WEDNESDAY SARA COULD HARDLY WAIT TO GET out of school. She quickly put on her red beret and her new spring coat with gold buttons. She raced across the schoolyard, her braids swinging in the breeze.

Rebecca ran after her. "Come and take a walk with me, Sara!" she yelled.

"I can't today. I've got to be home early. Margola is coming. I'll see you tomorrow!" Sara shouted back.

## A Gift for Mama

Usually in springtime Sara loved to walk with Rebecca through the streets of Vilna and through the marketplace near school. They would stop to smell the flowers in the flower stalls and to talk to the shopkeepers.

But this Wednesday, though it was warm and sunny, Sara ran straight home. She wanted to get her homework done before Margola came.

She took off her navy-blue smock uniform and put on her favorite old dotted dress. Then she began her homework. The arithmetic was as hard as ever, but book reports never gave Sara any trouble. She wrote one about *The Pious Cat* by I. L. Peretz in no time, and then she finished her assignment on the history of the old fortress in Vilna.

As soon as she finished all her homework, Sara took her favorite book in Polish, *Anne of Green Gables,* and went into the front hall to wait for Margola. She wanted to be sure that she would hear Margola's knock. Margola did not like to use the fancy doorbell Papa had installed. She often said the old-man door knocker would get lonely if no one used him.

Sara sat down on the bench. She had hardly had time to start her favorite chapter—the one in which Anne dyed her hair and it came out green—when she heard Margola's footsteps. She jumped up to open the door, even before Margola had a chance to knock.

"Well, Margola?"

"Well, Sara, let me come in first!" Margola dropped her books on the bench and hung up her coat and cap. Then she rubbed noses with Sara.

"Sara, I did think about your gift for Mama. I talked to your Uncle Eli and to Grandmother Hanna, too. We all feel that it isn't right to give you money to do something we know your mama wouldn't like. Remember, you said your papa would not want to help you do that either."

Margola and Sara went into the dining room. They pulled out chairs by the table. Margola moved hers close to Sara and put her arm around Sara's shoulders.

"Your Uncle Eli said maybe you could improve your grades in arithmetic as a gift to Mama! I told him to stop making fun of you." Margola smiled.

Sara was about to speak when Margola continued: "When we left your house on Monday, I spoke to my friends about your problem, too. Grisha thought you could borrow nine zlotys from Grandmother and pay it

back by not buying chocolates in the movies.''

Margola and Sara both laughed.

"I told him it would take you fifty years to pay it back," Margola went on. "I know my Sara could not watch a Shirley Temple movie without chocolates!''

"Oh, Margola, I'm sure I couldn't. How could I see Shirley Temple in *Heidi* without a whole box of chocolates? Chocolates keep me from crying too much. You know Rebecca and my other friends hate it when I cry at movies. They aren't like you or Mama and Papa. Besides, the chocolates from the movie candy lady are so delicious!''

"Well, Mira suggested that you write to Uncle Benjamin in America to send you money.'' Margola wrinkled her nose. "I told Mira that writing to rich relatives in America for favors, even to my own brother, was something we would not do. Grandmother would be furious if she ever heard I allowed you to ask him for money.''

Margola tossed her smooth black hair. She seemed furious herself at the suggestion.

"Oh, Margola, Mama would kill me if she ever found out I did something like that," Sara said.

"I think if your mama didn't kill you for asking Benjamin for money, she would certainly forbid you to go to the movies until you were old and gray!''

Sara and Margola threw their heads back and laughed. Sara went over to the sideboard. She brought the blue candy bowl to the table and took out some sour balls for Margola and herself.

"Well, let's see, Sara. Dina suggested that you make something you have never made before. Maybe a needlepoint bookmark?''

"No, Margola, this year I am not going to make anything. This year I am buying a present for Mama!''

Sara took a fruit-filled bonbon and munched on it.

"You know, Margola, this may sound dumb, but I had an idea of my own. Do you think I could become a clothes doctor for your friends?''

Margola smiled. Both her dimples showed. "A clothes doctor? What ever made you think of that?''

"When you were all here on Monday, I noticed that Grisha's and Janek's shirt collars were frayed. Mira's scarf was torn, and Bronia's stocking had a run. Dina's sweater needs elbow patches. You can almost see her bones! Sasha's left sock had the biggest hole I ever saw. I bet his foot froze in the winter.''

Sara rattled on. "I can darn socks and turn shirt collars and fix runs in stockings and make elbow patches and everything! You know that Mama and Grandmother Hanna taught me all that. If I become a clothes doctor, then I can earn money for Mama's present."

"Their clothes do look shabby," Margola said. "Many of my friends aren't from Vilna. They live not with their families but in rented rooms. They have a lot of homework and part-time jobs. You're right, Sara, their clothes do need fixing. I'll ask them tomorrow."

Sara took another piece of candy and gave one to Margola.

"When can you tell me what they say?"

"I'll tell you when Grandmother and Uncle Eli and I come to have dinner with you and Mama on Friday night."

"Thank you, Margolinka. You're the best aunt anyone ever had. And the smartest! And the youngest! And the prettiest!"

Sara put both arms around Margola's neck and kissed her on both cheeks, just where Margola had her dimples.

# Chapter IV

ON FRIDAY MAMA WAS VERY BUSY IN THE KITCHEN, preparing for the Sabbath. Grandmother bustled about, helping Mama. Sara and Margola came into the house almost at the same time, Sara from school and Margola from the university.

"Mama, did you hear from Papa today?" Sara asked. She was sorry that Papa was away. He loved Friday night dinners best of all.

"Yes, Papa called this morning to wish us a good Sabbath. He was invited to have dinner with some friends in Warsaw. I'm glad he won't be alone on Sabbath eve."

While the soup simmered on the stove and the chicken roasted in the oven, Mama and Grandmother prepared piroshki. Sara loved the meat-filled pastries that Mama made almost every Friday. Mama rolled out the dough on the wooden board and Grandmother cut it with a drinking glass into circles, just the right size to fill with chopped meat and onions.

"Mama, can Margola and I go to my room?" Sara was anxious to find out if Margola's friends had liked her plan.

"Not right now, Sara," Mama answered and turned to Margola.

"Margolinka, will you chop the onions for me, please? When I chop onions I cry and cry and cry!"

Margola knew that her big sister did not like to cry, not even when she chopped onions. She winked at Grandmother Hanna and at Sara. Sara did not wink back—she crossed her eyes and made a face.

"Sure, Raya, I'll chop the onions. But first give me a

few kitchen matches to put between my teeth. I've heard that match tips stop the tears,'' Margola answered.

"You, a chemistry major, you believe these old wives' tales?'' Mama looked at Margola with amusement. "But here are matches, anyway. They can't hurt, and maybe they'll help.''

As she chopped the onions, tears rolled down Margola's cheeks, despite the matches stuck between her teeth.

"You look like a weeping walrus,'' Sara said.

"Only much prettier,'' added Grandmother Hanna as she wiped the tears from Margola's face with the edge of her big white apron. She and Mama laughed.

"Mama, Margola's finished with the onions. Can we go to my room for a little while now?'' Sara asked impatiently.

"After you buff the Sabbath candlesticks with the flannel mitt you made,'' Mama answered evenly.

"Can't I do it in my room? Please, Mama. Margola can watch me. Then I'll take them to the dining room. All right?''

Sara was determined to get away from the kitchen with Margola.

"All right," Mama said. "But first get a piece of newspaper to put on your desk while you buff the candlesticks."

*Fussy, fussy,* Sara whispered to herself. But she took a piece of old newspaper, the pair of tall silver candlesticks, and the yellow flannel mitt. Sara slammed the door to her room with the heel of her foot and turned to Margola.

"Did you talk to your friends? What did they say? Can I be their clothes doctor?"

"Yes, Sara, I spoke to them. They think your idea is wonderful! Grisha said he will give you a degree of Doctor of Fixing Torn Socks and Frayed Collars, but I said he should wait till you do all the work."

Sara sighed with relief. She buffed the candlesticks with great vigor, back and forth, back and forth, until they shone like mirrors.

"To earn nine zlotys, you will have to turn four shirt collars for Grisha and three collars for Janek. And Sasha has six socks with holes. Mira's scarf needs mending and Dina said that elbow patches on her sweater would be just right. Bronia has two pairs of silk stockings with runs in each one. Do you really think you can do all that in less than two weeks? Wouldn't you rather make a gift for Mama?"

"No, Margola, I don't want to make a gift. I want to buy a gift. I'm old enough to earn money. And Mama said she'd wear the beautiful black satin robe when she had new slippers."

Sara twisted the yellow flannel mitt in her hands.

"Tell your friends that I can start on Monday. You just bring all their things to your house. I'll do it there."

Sara knew that Mama would not mind her visiting at Grandmother Hanna's house after school.

"You know, Margola, Mama may even think I'm making her a gift in your house. Will she ever be surprised when I give her the slippers!"

Sara and Margola carried the candlesticks to the dining-room table. It was growing dim outside—it was almost time to light the Sabbath candles. Soon Uncle Eli would come and they would all sit down to a festive Sabbath eve dinner.

Grandmother and Mama came in, without their aprons, wearing fine silk blouses and dark skirts.

Mama put the short white candles in the candlesticks. She and Grandmother put some coins into the charity

box. Sara struck a match for Mama. Mama and Grand-mother put white scarves on their heads and made circles over the burning candles with their hands. And they said the Sabbath prayers, just as they did every Friday night.

Sara added her own silent prayer, *Please, please let everything work out well with my gift for Mama.*

# *Chapter V*

RIGHT AFTER SCHOOL ON MONDAY, BEFORE GOING TO
Grandmother Hanna's house, Sara went to the Bata Shoe
Store on Broad Street. It was raining. Sara carried her
big red umbrella. The wind kept turning it inside out.

She stopped in front of the shoe store window and
looked for the slippers. They were not there! She could
not believe her eyes. She moved the umbrella back and
leaned closer to the window. Still she did not see the

slippers. Sara took out her handkerchief and wiped the raindrops off the window. She looked from shoe to shoe, from boot to boot, from one slipper to another. But the shiny black satin slippers with the blue leather trim were gone.

Sara closed her umbrella and went into the store. There were no customers. An elderly bald man with steel-rimmed glasses stood near the cashier's counter. Sara walked over to him.

"Excuse me, sir, I want to buy the black satin slippers with the blue leather trim for my mother. They were in your window about two weeks ago. They aren't there now, but I remember they cost nine zlotys. My friend Rebecca and I saw them. They were in the middle of the window display, and they were so pretty . . ."

Sara's voice trailed off and tears started to well up in her eyes.

"Well, my dear, the owner of the store decided to take them out of the window because there are very few left in stock. But tell me, what size do you need?"

Sara was stunned. She had never thought of finding out her mother's shoe size.

"I don't know," Sara mumbled.

"Let's see now, has your mother ever bought shoes here before?"

"Oh, yes," said Sara. "She bought a pair of brown pumps here a while ago, and also a pair of party patent leather shoes for me."

"Well, let's see what we can do," said the salesman. "What is your mother's name? I'll look it up in our records and see what size she wears."

Sara nearly kissed the salesman. "My mother's name is Raya Domin."

While the salesman went to the back of the store to check, Sara looked around. Many of the slippers displayed on the shelves cost much less than nine zlotys. Some were very pretty. But the black satin slippers with the blue leather trim were the most beautiful slippers of all.

The salesman returned. "Your mother wears size thirty-eight shoes," he said. "And the slippers that were in the window are still in the store."

"What size are they?" Sara whispered.

"Thirty-eight," replied the salesman with a big smile.

"Oh, thank you, thank you!" Sara stretched out her arms to hug the salesman, but dropped them to her sides in sudden embarrassment.

"You know, sir, I don't have the money today. Could you put the slippers away until the Friday before Mother's Day? By then I'll have nine zlotys to pay for them."

"I really shouldn't do it," he said. "According to store rules, you must give me a deposit of at least one quarter of the price of the shoes."

"How much will that be, sir? I'm really very bad in arithmetic."

The salesman replied, "Well, a quarter of nine zlotys should be two zlotys and twenty-five groszy, my dear."

"But, sir, I don't even have the twenty-five groszy now!"

"Let's see," said the salesman. "I know your family's name. I pass your father's business, The S. Domin House of Trade, every day. I bought a small refrigerator there last year. Your mother has bought shoes here before. I think the store rules can be bent a little—yes, I do. I will put your name on the shoe box and save the slippers for you."

"Oh, thank you! You promise that these slippers will not be sold to anyone?"

"I promise," said the salesman.

The rain had stopped when Sara left the Bata Shoe Store to go to Grandmother Hanna's house. She walked down Broad Street, one of the busiest streets in Vilna. Many of the finest stores were there. The biggest bookstore was right next to the Bata Shoe Store. Sara often went in to look at new books and to make lists of those she wanted.

She passed by Cinema Mars, but did not stop to look at the announcements of coming attractions. Today Sara had no time to look in the bookstore or to think about movies. She knew she had a lot of work waiting for her. She hurried along Broad Street to Grandmother Hanna's house.

As soon as Grandmother let her in, she dropped her school bag, coat, and umbrella and went straight to Grandmother's bedroom. The mending basket was stuffed to the very top. The shirts from Grisha and Janek, Sasha's socks, Dina's sweater, Mira's scarf, and Bronia's stockings were all there. There certainly was a lot of work piled up for Sara.

Grandmother followed her and kissed the top of Sara's head.

"My, you're in a hurry today. No time to kiss your grandmother?"

Sara put her arms around Grandmother Hanna's waist and rested her head against Grandmother's plump arm.

"I'm sorry, Grandmother. I wanted to be sure all my work was here. I was so upset before I got here. You see, I went to the Bata Shoe Store and the slippers weren't in the window. I thought I'd die!"

"You don't die from slippers missing in a shoe store window. But I'm sure you were in tears." Grandmother patted Sara's head. "What happened?"

"Well, it's a long story, but everything is all right now. The salesman put away the slippers. I can pick them up on Friday before Mother's Day. And guess what? He let me put them away without a deposit!"

"Good, good, my child. Do you want some cocoa? You must have gotten chilled in the rain."

"No, no, Grandmother," Sara answered. "I have such a lot of work. I'd like your sewing basket and the darning egg, please. I didn't bring my own." She reached into the mending basket and pulled out Sasha's sock.

Grandmother handed Sara the sewing basket and the darning egg and smiled. "You know, Sara, I hope Mama won't mind that you aren't making her a gift this year."

Sara did not even look up from her work to answer Grandmother; she was too busy. The darning needle with the yarn was moving swiftly in her strong hands.

# Chapter VI

FOR THE NEXT TWO WEEKS SARA WENT STRAIGHT FROM school to Grandmother Hanna's house. Rebecca couldn't understand it. Sara wouldn't go with her to play at the old fortress. She wouldn't go for walks in the market-place, either, or on Broad Street, or through the Berna-diner Garden, just when all the daffodils and tulips were beginning to bloom.

"What do you do at your grandmother's house every afternoon, Sara?" Rebecca asked.

"I can't tell you. It's a secret."

Rebecca did not nag her. She knew that Sara could keep a secret better than any of her other friends. But she was disappointed, and she told Sara, "I never see you any more. Whatever you're doing, I hope it ends soon."

"Sometimes I do, too," Sara answered, because she missed her friends and the work was boring and hard and there was so much of it. But she did need those nine zlotys!

One warm afternoon in early May Grandmother said to Sara, "You know, I especially love this time of year! It brings back so many happy memories of your Grandfather Hillel."

Sara looked up from mending the run in Bronia's stocking. It was painstakingly slow work to use the little hooked needle to pick up the tiny stitches in the stocking.

"Why especially this time of year, Grandmother?"

"Well, you know, Sara, Grandfather traded in timber, and spring was usually a very busy time for him. He enjoyed his work, and he just loved being busy! He planted seedlings. He also cut down trees and made them

into logs and built the finest rafts to send down the river.''

"I bet Mama loved to go and see Grandfather Hillel cut the logs and build the rafts,'' Sara said. She blinked and bent her head again to work on Bronia's stocking.

"Oh, no, Sara, your mama didn't like it at all. Your mama loved sweets, just like you! Her best friend's father had a candy factory. Now *that* was the most wonderful business to be in, your mama thought. She and her friend would visit the candy factory and eat all the sweets they wanted. When she was little, your mama complained that it wasn't any fun to have a father in the lumber business. She'd ask, 'Can I eat wood when I go to visit him?' ''

"Well, I love to visit my papa's business, and I can't eat any of the machinery and equipment he sells.'' Sara laughed. "So maybe Mama wasn't just like me when she was little!''

Sara's face grew serious. "Tell me, Grandmother, did Mama cry a lot when she was young?''

"No, no, Sara, your mama hardly ever cried. When she was sad, she would get very quiet. When she was mad at me or her father or her brothers, Benjamin and Eli, she'd get the shovel and take it to the garden and dig a hole near her favorite lilac bush. She said that if she dug deep enough, she'd get to China and leave us all in Vilna. Then we'd miss her and be sorry we were mean to her.''

Grandmother threw her head back and laughed so hard her whole body shook. Sara looked up from her work, astonished. Mama didn't like to travel now, not even in their new car, but when she was little she'd wanted to go all the way to China through a hole in the garden!

"Uncle Eli said China wasn't on the opposite side of the world from Vilna. Mama said it was. Oh, how they'd argue!" Grandmother sighed.

"Your Uncle Benjamin said he would get to America before she ever got to China. And, of course, he did— before your mama went anywhere, let alone to China.''

"What did Grandfather say when Mama dug the hole?''

"Grandfather promised your mama that if she would stop digging, he would send her to Paris when she got older, to become a real artist.''

Sara's work lay quite still in her lap as she looked at Grandmother's face.

"Oh, Mama must have loved to hear that!''

"Yes, she did! She wanted so much to become an artist and to study in Paris. But then Grandfather Hillel died and Benjamin went to America. Eli was very young, and Margola was just a little baby. And Mama never went to Paris—or to China."

Grandmother Hanna got up from her chair and went over to Sara. Sara reached for Grandmother's hand.

"It's sad that Mama never got to study art in Paris," Sara said softly. Grandmother put her fingers on Sara's cheek.

"Yes, yes, Sara, that's the way life goes. But Mama always did paint and draw and make beautiful things out of clay. When she was young, Mama made gifts for everyone in the family."

"I know, Grandmother, I know. Maybe that's why she always wants me to make gifts. And I have, haven't I? But not this year. This year I am *buying* her a present!"

Sara picked up Bronia's stocking and finished mending the run.

There were times when Sara was afraid she would never finish, but by the Thursday before Mother's Day she had mended the sweater, the scarf, and all the socks. She had turned all the shirt collars and fixed the runs in all the stockings. Sara folded them all neatly and put them on Grandmother's bed.

Margola's friends came to get their things late Thursday afternoon. Janek unfolded one of his shirts.

"Sara, are you sure you didn't make me an entirely new shirt? This looks wonderful!"

"Stop teasing me, Janek. You know perfectly well it's your old shirt!" But Sara was pleased.

Grisha took off his university cap and put it on Sara's head.

"Sara, now I officially name you Doctor of Fixing Torn Socks and Frayed Collars."

Everyone liked Sara's work. They paid her right away. Now Sara had nine zlotys to pay for Mama's slippers, and she had earned it all herself!

Sara went to the Bata Shoe Store on Friday after school. Papa was returning from Warsaw, and she knew that Mama would be meeting him at the railroad station. No one would be there when she got home so she could easily hide the slippers.

She took the money from her coat pocket and counted it three times. Then she went inside the store. The nice salesman was there.

"Sir, I have the nine zlotys for the slippers."

"I was sure you would, my dear." He smiled.

When the salesman brought her the box, Sara asked for a plain white card.

"Happy Mother's Day with love from Sara," she wrote. She did not even draw a flower or a smiling face on it. But she smiled to herself. *All store-bought, and a store card, too,* she thought with satisfaction.

# Chapter VII

O<small>N</small> S<small>UNDAY</small> M<small>ORNING</small> S<small>ARA</small> K<small>NOCKED</small> O<small>N</small> H<small>ER</small>
parents' bedroom door.

"Come in," Mama said.

Sara opened the door slowly. Mama was wearing her
old red flannel robe. She sat before the mirror at the
dressing table, braiding her long black hair and arranging
it in a large bun at the back of her neck. Papa sat in bed,
reading *Gone with the Wind* in Polish.

"Here, Mama, Happy Mother's Day to you." Sara handed the shoe box to Mama and leaned against the dressing table.

Mama looked surprised. She opened the box slowly and looked inside. Then she looked at Sara. She looked inside the box again.

"Thank you very much," Mama said quietly.

"I did not make a present for you this year. I bought one."

"Yes, I see," Mama answered.

"I'm sure it's lovely, Sara," Papa said with a big smile. "Tell me what it is." He closed the book.

"I bought Mama slippers to go with her shiny black satin robe, Papa," Sara answered. She waited.

"Isn't that a nice surprise!" Papa said.

Sara hoped that Mama would put on the black satin robe and the beautiful black satin slippers and walk into the dining room looking like a movie star. But Mama put on her old scuffed red slippers. And she was still wearing the red flannel robe when she left the bedroom to make breakfast.

Sara's eyes filled with tears, but she was determined not to cry.

## A Gift for Mama

*Too bad for Mama,* Sara said to herself.

"Come here, Sara." Papa patted the edge of the bed. "Let me tell you about the opera Mama and I heard last night. It was about an artist named Cavaradossi who was in love with an actress named Tosca, and they had all this trouble with a man named Scarpia. Oh, did they have trouble!"

Papa clicked his tongue. "But they did sing the most beautiful music all evening long."

Sara did not move from Mama's dressing table. She was in no mood to listen to some dumb story about an artist who loved an actress and to hear about their troubles. She had enough of her own.

"Let me tell you the whole story, Sara, and I'll sing some of the arias for you, too," Papa said. He patted the edge of his bed again.

"Thanks, Papa, but not now. Maybe later."

"All right, Sara. But how about a big hug and kiss from your papa?"

"Sure, Papa." Sara went over to his bed. Papa gave her a big kiss on her forehead as she bent over him. But Sara's hands were clasped tightly behind her back, and she did not smile.

On Mother's Day in the afternoon, Margola, Uncle Eli, and Grandmother Hanna came to visit. Only children gave presents to their mothers, but most families in Vilna celebrated this special day.

The dining room table was covered with a lace tablecloth that Mama had crocheted. A big bowl of lilacs was in the middle of the table. Mama put out platters of cake, cookies, candy, and fruit. She set out the silver samovar for making tea. Sara did not help. She sat in her favorite chair and read a magazine.

The doorbell rang. Margola opened the door. Sasha and Grisha, Janek and Mira, Bronia and Dina rushed into the dining room.

"Surprise!" they shouted.

Although it was quite warm, Mira wore the scarf that Sara had fixed, and Dina wore her sweater. Bronia wore the silk stockings without any runs in them. Grisha and Janek wore shirts on which Sara had turned the collars. Sasha sat down in the doorway, took off his shoe and raised his leg. Mama was so surprised she did not say a word.

"See, Raya," Sasha said to Mama, "Sara darned this

sock for me to earn money for your slippers. Isn't this the best darning you ever saw?''

Mama bent over Sasha's foot and examined his sock. "Oh, yes, it is wonderful darning," she said, looking at Sara.

Grisha took off his jacket. Then he took off his shirt and handed it to Mama.

"Isn't this the most neatly turned shirt collar you have ever seen, Raya? Sara turned four collars for me to earn money.''

"And three for me," added Janek.

Mama went over to Sara, put her arms around Sara's shoulders, and rested her chin on Sara's head.

Mira asked, "Raya, can you tell that my scarf had a huge rip? Sara mended it for me!''

"No, I can't tell at all!''

Mama buried her face in Sara's hair. She did not look up for a very long time. Sara did not move or say a word. At last Mama raised her head, swallowed hard, and smiled.

Then everyone was talking at once, showing Mama again all the things that Sara had fixed to earn money for

the slippers. Mama went around the room and admired everything.

"Sara, this morning you said that you did not make my gift this year," Mama whispered in Sara's ear, "but you did all this work!"

"I did not *make* a gift for you, Mama. This year I earned money to *buy* a gift for you!" Sara whispered back and put her arms around Mama.

"Excuse me for a minute." Mama left the dining room.

Sara wondered why Mama did not go to the kitchen to get more cake and cookies and lemon for the tea. Instead Mama went to her bedroom, on the other side of the apartment. Soon Mama returned wearing her black satin robe and the black satin slippers trimmed in blue. Sara could hardly believe her eyes. Mama put on a robe and slippers in the middle of the afternoon!

Margola saluted Sara, and Uncle Eli looked as pleased as if Sara had suddenly done the whole multiplication table without a single mistake. Grandmother Hanna grinned from ear to ear.

Mama sat down at the dining room table and served everyone. She looked just like a movie star. Sara wanted to cry, this time because she was so happy. Instead she smiled. There were tears in Papa's eyes. Everyone else laughed and joked. And they all had lots of cake and fruit and tea with lemon and sugar.

ABOUT THE BOOK

The illustrations for *A Gift for Mama* were created by the monoprint technique. The artist painted each picture on glass or mylar, using oil-based inks, then transferred it onto paper by running the plate through an etching press. Only one impression can be pulled from each plate, therefore the name monoprint.

The text type is Times Roman. The display type is Centaur.